W9-AAM-579

e story of

Walter the Whale with Wings

Edward Lahti

llustrated with Melissa Frost

the story of Walter the Whale with Wings

Copyright © 2013 by Edward Lahti

All rights reserved. No part of this book may be reproduced or transmitted in any form or by any means without written permission of the author.

Illustrations by: Melissa Frost and Edward Lahti
Jacket design by: Jacob Kubon
Author Photo by: Jennifer Atwood
Author Bio by: Quincy Gow

Published by: Splattered Ink Press

splatteredinkpress.com

ISBN: 978-1-939294-09-8

The Story of Walter the Whale with Wings

For Uriah.

One Wednesday, Walter the Whale wondered what it would be like to have wings.

Walter wandered, wavering in the water
a while, when he came upon a fish.

This fish was in a bit of a fix,
so Walter inquired to see if he could assist.

The fish did insist, with a fin flailing swish, and promised a wish as a gift, if Walter could assist.

Walter was astonished that a fish could grant a wish, so after freeing the fish from its fix, he asked how the fish could do this.

This fish was no ordinary fish; this fish was a wizard fish.

Well, Walter wanted to know why the wizard wasn't waving a wand. The fish replied that he was a winking wizard fish!

With the blink of an eye, the fishy wizard would grant a wish, and Walter found this quite curious.

Walter had to think and asked the fish if he could reserve his winked wish.

The fish agreed, and gave Walter the whale a while to decide what he wanted.

Walter wandered through the waters wondering what a wonderful world it would be, if he were a whale, a whale with wings.

The next day, Walter returned to the fish and asked for his wish, the wish for wings.

The fish wanted to know if Walter was serious. So Walter said with a smile that he had thought for a while, and this is what he wanted.

With the wink of the eye of the wizard fish,
Walter was no longer a whale.

He was now a whale with WINGS!

The wizard and Walter laughed, and the wizard fish then asked Walter what he would do now that he was the whale with wings.

Walter looked up and replied, with a wink in his eye, that it was time to fly. Fly high in the big, beautiful, blue sky.

Loppu

the end